BROWNIE GROUNDHOG
and the WINTRY SURPRISE

By
Susan Blackaby

Illustrated by
Carmen Segovia

STERLING CHILDREN'S BOOKS
New York

On a December afternoon, Brownie Groundhog and
her friend the fox shared their picnic with a new friend,
Bunny. A thin crust of ice rimmed the rocks around
the pond.

The fox picked crumbs out of his fur.
"Perfect picnic, Brownie," he said. "What's next?"

Brownie yawned. "Naptime." She wound her scarf
around her neck. "I'm going home to sleep until spring."

"Already?" The fox's chin quivered.
"What about me?"

"You'll be fine," said Brownie. Each word puffed out of her mouth on a tiny cloud. "You can do wintry things." Brownie packed up her basket. "Just don't wake me up. And don't eat Bunny. She's company."

A few days later, Bunny bumped
into the fox, moping along the path.

"You seem blue," said Bunny.

"I am." The fox felt whiny. "It's so cold."

"Move faster," Bunny suggested. "Try to trit-trot."

She zigzagged, lippety lippety, over the frosty ground.

"Can't." The fox slumped against a stump. "I'm too sad from no Brownie and nothing to do."
Bunny draped the fox's tail around her shoulders.
"Too bad your tail can't reach your neck," she said. "Then you'd have a snug scarf for doing wintry things."
The fox sighed. "A cozy red one," he said. "Just like Brownie's."
"No fair," said Bunny. "She doesn't even need hers. She's sleeping."
"That's right!" said the fox, suddenly cheerful. "Let's go borrow Brownie's scarf!"

"Are you sure this is a good idea?" asked Bunny
as they crept into Brownie's house.

"Positive," said the fox. He leaned over the bump in the bed. "Hello-o," he said. "May I borrow your scarf?"

Brownie's answer came out sounding slurry and drowsy. "Beaky white, yam slippy," she said. "Doony dizzer!"

Bunny tugged the fox toward the door. "Let's go," Bunny whispered. "Brownie just said, 'Be quiet, I'm sleeping! Do not disturb!'"

"Nuh-uh," said the fox. "She wants me to look in the dresser. But don't worry. I'll be extra quiet."

The fox spotted Brownie's scarf and a wooly
sweater. Then he reeled out strings of lights. "Ooh,"
he said, hatching a plan. "These'll be great! We can
use them for looping and twinkling!"

"How?" asked Bunny.

"Hmmm." The fox scratched his ear. Then he gave the Brownie bump a nudge. "Pssst," he said. "Is it okay if we grab a ladder?"

Brownie sounded fuzzy and muzzy.

"Gooey wave! Stop blobbery bee!" She snuggled deeper under her quilt.

"We need to leave." Bunny's eyes were as bright as buttons. "Brownie said, 'Go away and stop bothering me!'"

"No, no. Brownie said, 'Go ahead and use whatever you need.'"

The fox rummaged in the closet, thumping and bumping, clattering and clanking.

"What's this stuff for?"
asked Bunny, loading up a
wheelbarrow.

"You'll see," said the fox.
He waggled Brownie's shoulder.

"Excuse me," he said. "Hammer?"
Brownie sat up, groggy and foggy.
"Bumble crumpet! Lemon sheep!"

"Did she say 'trumpet'?" The fox clapped. "**A** trumpet would be terrific."

"No," said Bunny. "She said, 'Let me sleep.' She sounds kind of mad."

"Silly," said the fox. "She's not mad. She's sleeping."

The fox jumbled in the cupboards, hunting and grunting. "Lucky us!" he said. "**A** hammer and a trumpet!"

When the fox had everything he needed, he teetered the wheelbarrow down the path. Bunny trooped along behind, scooping up whatever spilled. Then they got to work.

They twisted and twined,

decked and draped,

wrapped and snapped.

The front door flew open.

"HEY!" Brownie was wide awake.

"Well, hi!" said the fox. "You're up early."

"What do you think you're doing?" snapped Brownie.

"A wintry thing." The fox pointed at the wreath.

"Sorry about the noise," said Bunny.

"It isn't really noise," said the fox, steering Brownie out the door. "It's more of a . . ."

Bunny tootled on the trumpet while the fox beat the drum. They marched three times around the tree so that Brownie could admire it from every angle.

"A wintry surprise!" said Brownie. "So jolly! What else have you got?"

"We've got the hungries," said the fox. "Let's fix a wintry surprise holiday feast."

Bunny nodded. "With pie," she said.

Around Brownie's table, the candles glowed. There were streamers and poppers, crackers, and snappers. The fox passed out presents, and everyone put on party hats. They dangled spoons from their noses and sang songs and giggled until they got the hiccups. Bunny slurped three helpings of carrot soup, and the fox stuffed himself with stuffing.

"I've never been to a holiday feast before," said Brownie,
"but this was the best ever."
Everyone agreed.
Outside, the first big snowfall of the season blanketed the
path. Brownie stretched, happy and dozy. "Time for sleep,"
she said.

"Sweet dreams," said Bunny.
"See you in February," said the fox.
"And not one second sooner," said Brownie,
and she shuffled off to bed.

When the dishes were put away, Bunny and the fox tiptoed out
of the house. Moonlight glowed on the snow, and the lights twinkled
in the tree.

"That was nice," said the fox, "but I wish we had a little more pie."

"SURPRISE!" said Bunny.

And they ate up every crumb.

For my brother, Jim, who loved surprises. ~S.B.

For my Mexican family, a precious gift. ~C.S.

STERLING CHILDREN'S BOOKS
New York

An Imprint of Sterling Publishing
387 Park Avenue South
New York, NY 10016

STERLING CHILDREN'S BOOKS and the distinctive Sterling Children's Books logo are trademarks of Sterling Publishing Co., Inc.

Text © 2013 by Susan Blackaby
Illustrations © 2013 by Carmen Segovia
Designed by Merideth Harte

ISBN 978-1-4027-9836-8

The artwork for this book was created using acrylic paint and ink.
The story is based on a character created by Carmen Segovia.

Distributed in Canada by Sterling Publishing
c/o Canadian Manda Group, 165 Dufferin Street
Toronto, Ontario, Canada M6K 3H6
Distributed in the United Kingdom by GMC Distribution Services
Castle Place, 166 High Street, Lewes, East Sussex, England BN7 1XU
Distributed in Australia by Capricorn Link (Australia) Pty. Ltd.
P.O. Box 704, Windsor, NSW 2756, Australia

For information about custom editions, special sales, and premium and corporate purchases, please contact
Sterling Special Sales at 800-805-5489 or specialsales@sterlingpublishing.com.

Printed in China
Lot #:
2 4 6 8 10 9 7 5 3 1
04/13

www.sterlingpublishing.com/kids